This book belongs to

_____

_____

Copyright © 2018 Disney/Pixar. All rights reserved.

Published by Scholastic Australia in 2018.

Scholastic Australia Pty Limited
PO Box 579 Gosford NSW 2250
ABN 11 000 614 577
www.scholastic.com.au

Part of the Scholastic Group
Sydney • Auckland • New York • Toronto • London • Mexico City
New Delhi • Hong Kong • Buenos Aires • Puerto Rico

All rights reserved. No part of this publication may be reproduced or transmitted in any form or by any means,
electronic or mechanical, including photocopying, recording, storage in an information retrieval system,
or otherwise, without the prior written permission of the publisher, unless specifically permitted under the
Australian Copyright Act 1968 as amended.

ISBN 978-1-76066-398-8

Printed in China by Hang Tai Printing Company Limited.

Scholastic Australia's policy, in association with Hang Tai, is to use papers that are renewable and made
efficiently from wood grown in responsibly managed forests, so as to minimise its environmental footprint.

10 9 8 7 6 5 4 3 2   18 19 20 21 22 / 1

DISNEY · PIXAR

CLASSIC COLLECTION

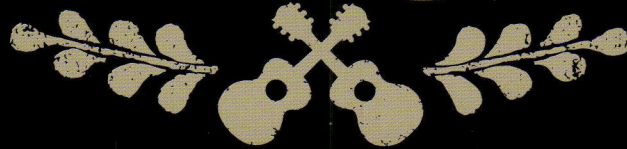

COCO

SCHOLASTIC
SYDNEY AUCKLAND NEW YORK TORONTO LONDON MEXICO CITY
NEW DELHI HONG KONG BUENOS AIRES PUERTO RICO

Many years ago, in a tiny town called Santa Cecilia, a little girl named Coco lived with her parents. Coco's home was full of music and dancing. But one day, her father left to follow a dream of music.

Coco's mother, Mamá Imelda, needed money for food and clothes, so she learned how to make shoes. Her business did well and her family grew. But she would not speak about Coco's father. She tore his face out of the family photo, and she would have no music in the Rivera household.

Coco grew up and had a family of her own, with many grandchildren and great-grandchildren. One of them was called Miguel, and he dreamed of being a musician, just like his idol, Ernesto de la Cruz. But Miguel's dream was a secret because of the old family rule: NO MUSIC!

Miguel wished he could tell his Mamá Coco that music made him happier than anything. But he could only share his secret with a street dog called Dante.

The Rivera family were shoemakers,
and everyone worked in the family business
when they grew up. Miguel's grandmother
Elena was the head of the family. He needed
her permission to be a musician, but the family
rule was very important to her. In fact, everything
about family was important to her. Miguel didn't
dare to tell her how he felt.

On the day before Día de los Muertos, Elena
filled his arms with marigolds.

'Tonight is about family,' she said.

Mamá Coco listened as Elena told Miguel why Día de los Muertos was such a special celebration.

'This is the one night of the year when our ancestors can visit us,' she said.

She explained that when their ancestors' photos were placed on the ofrenda altar, their spirits could cross over to the Land of the Living. Marigold petals would help the spirits find their way.

Later, in his attic hideout, Miguel strummed his
secret guitar and watched an old de la Cruz film.
Ernesto de la Cruz was dead, but Miguel had loved
his music for as long as he could remember.

'When you see your moment, you must seize it,'
said the singer.

'I've got to seize my moment!' Miguel cried.

Miguel raced off to tell his grandmother that he wanted to be
a musician. But on the way, Dante accidentally smashed a family
ofrenda photo frame. Miguel unfolded the torn photo inside,
and his heart leaped with excitement. The man in the photo was
holding de la Cruz's guitar.

'Mamá Coco's father was Ernesto de la Cruz!' Miguel exclaimed.

Miguel could hardly wait to tell his family the news.
But instead of being excited, they were furious. Elena
grabbed his precious guitar and smashed it to pieces.

Shocked and hurt, Miguel ran from his house. There was a talent show in the plaza, and he longed to join in. But he couldn't take part without a guitar. Miguel had never felt so alone.

'Great-great-grandfather, what am I supposed to do?' he asked.

Suddenly, a wonderful idea came to him. He hurried to de la Cruz's tomb and crept inside. The musician's famous guitar was hanging on the wall.

'I need to borrow this,' Miguel whispered.

He lifted it off the wall and strummed a chord. Suddenly, glowing marigold petals started to swirl around him. He felt strangely dizzy.

The door flew open and the groundsman rushed in. 'Who's in there?' he called.

Miguel tried to explain, but the man walked straight through him!

Miguel raced out of the tomb and fell straight into an open grave. He took the hand of a kind woman who offered to help him out, only to realise she was a skeleton! There were skeletons everywhere! Worse still, living people couldn't see him. Only Dante could see Miguel. What had happened to him?

In his panic, Miguel bumped into more skeletons, and these ones knew his name. They were his ancestors.

Miguel felt calmer. Even though they were dead, these people were his family. He could trust them. They decided to take him to the Land of the Dead.

'Mamá Imelda will know what to do,' they said.

Miguel and Dante walked across a glowing bridge of
marigold petals, which led from the Land of the Living to the
beautiful Land of the Dead. Flying creatures of all shapes and
sizes zoomed around the sparkling buildings. Miguel's family
told him that they were the spirit guides of the dead.

A skeleton called Héctor was trying to cross the bridge.
But no-one had put a photo on an ofrenda, so he could not get across.

Miguel forgot about Héctor when he found Mamá Imelda. She was annoyed because she hadn't been able to cross into the Land of the Living. When Miguel explained that it was because he had taken her photo from the ofrenda, she was absolutely furious.

Miguel had been cursed because
he had taken the guitar from the tomb.
To get home, he needed his family's
blessing before sunrise. Without it,
he would turn into a skeleton forever.

Mamá Imelda held up a marigold petal, which started to glow.
'I give you my blessing to go home,' she said, but then she added
a condition. 'Put my photo back on the ofrenda and never play
music again.'
Miguel was shocked. He couldn't promise that!

Miguel and Dante slipped away from Mamá Imelda.

'I need a musician's blessing,' Miguel said. 'We've got to find my great-great-grandpa!'

Just then, Miguel overheard the skeleton called Héctor boasting that he knew Ernesto de la Cruz.

Miguel made a deal with him. Héctor would help Miguel to get his great-great-grandpa's blessing. In return, Miguel would put a photo of Héctor on his family ofrenda. Then Héctor would be able to cross the Marigold Bridge to the Land of the Living.

Héctor helped Miguel to disguise himself as a skeleton, then they hurried to de la Cruz's show, the Sunrise Spectacular. But the singer wasn't in the rehearsal area.

'Ernesto doesn't do rehearsals,' said an artist called Frida. 'He's too busy hosting that fancy party at the top of his tower.'

Miguel needed to get into that party. Luckily, there was a contest in the plaza, and the winner would perform at de la Cruz's party. It was Miguel's best chance, but he was going to need a guitar.

Héctor remembered that his friend Chicharrón had a guitar. But poor Chicharrón had begun to fade. Héctor played a song to comfort him as he vanished into dust.

'When there's no-one left in the living world who remembers you, you disappear from this world,' Héctor explained. 'We call it the Final Death.' He handed Miguel the guitar. 'Come on, you've got a contest to win.'

Miguel performed at the contest and the audience went wild. But meanwhile, his ancestors had been looking for him. They asked the announcer on stage to tell everyone to look out for a living boy. Miguel was trapped. They had found him!

Miguel tried to get away, but Mamá Imelda spotted him.
'I am giving you my blessing and you are going home,' she said.
'I don't want your blessing!' Miguel cried.
He couldn't let her send him home without music. Through all his adventures, it was still the most important wish in his heart. Why wouldn't his family let him follow his heart?
'Family should support you,' he said. 'But you never will.'

Miguel ran to de la Cruz's tower and climbed to the top of the grand staircase. There was a crowd of people below, and he could see de la Cruz. He knew what he had to do. Miguel began to play, and the crowd fell silent. He walked towards Ernesto de la Cruz, strumming and singing.

Just as he reached de la Cruz, Miguel tripped and fell into the pool.

'You are that boy,' the musician exclaimed. 'The one who came from the Land of the Living.'

Miguel realised that the water had washed the disguise away from his face. It was time to tell his idol who he was.

Ernesto de la Cruz was thrilled to find out that he was Miguel's great-great-grandfather. He lifted Miguel onto his shoulders for all the crowd to see.

'You, my great-great-grandson, are meant to be a musician!' announced de la Cruz proudly.

Knowing he was running out of time,
Miguel asked for de la Cruz's blessing.
But at that moment, Héctor found them.
'You said you'd take back my photo,'
he said. 'You promised, Miguel.'
He held out the photo of himself.
Suddenly he looked pale and weak.

'My friend,' de la Cruz murmured, recognising the man in the picture. 'You're . . . you're being forgotten.'

'And whose fault is that?' said Héctor. 'Those were my songs you took. My songs that made you famous.'

Miguel gasped. Could this be true?

Héctor told Miguel that when he was alive, he had been a songwriter. He had left his family to play music with de la Cruz, and then he had changed his mind. He had wanted to go home. But de la Cruz had decided to get rid of Héctor and steal his songs.

'You poisoned me!' Héctor cried.
He tried to grab de la Cruz, but
guards dragged him away.

Miguel was trembling. Why had his idol done such a terrible thing? And would de la Cruz still send Miguel back home, now that the boy knew about Héctor? De la Cruz folded Héctor's photo and put it in his pocket.

'You were going to give me your blessing,' said Miguel, feeling his heart thumping in his chest.

De la Cruz looked at him . . . and then called the guards to take him away.

'But I'm your family!' Miguel cried.

'And Héctor was my best friend,' said de la Cruz, watching as the guards threw Miguel into a deep pit.

Miguel found Héctor in the pit.

'She's forgetting me,' Héctor said.
'My daughter. My Coco.'

He sounded as if his heart would break.
Miguel's head was spinning. He pulled his family's
ofrenda photo out of his pocket.

'That's my Mamá Coco,' he said, pointing
at the picture of his great-grandmother.

'We're . . . family?' said Héctor.

He told Miguel that de la Cruz's most famous song, 'Remember Me', was a lullaby he had written for Coco, so she wouldn't forget him while he was away. Miguel smiled at Héctor, full of pride and love.

Just then, Dante's friendly face peered into the pit. He had helped Pepita, Mamá Imelda's spirit guide, to find them. Miguel's heart swelled when he realised that Dante was more than just an ordinary dog. He was a true spirit guide. Pepita swooped down and they climbed on her back.

Pepita carried them to a nearby plaza, where the rest of Miguel's ancestors were waiting. Mamá Imelda looked at Héctor, her long-lost husband. He was still fading away. Soon he would be gone forever.

'It's Coco,' she said. 'She's forgetting you.'

Miguel couldn't let that happen to Héctor. He had to get the photo back from de la Cruz. When Mamá Imelda heard what had happened all those years ago, she agreed to help.

At the Sunrise Spectacular, Miguel and his family chased de la Cruz. The singer's guards tried to catch them, but Mamá Imelda grabbed Héctor's photo. Suddenly, the stage began to rise.

'Sing!' cried Miguel.

Mamá Imelda's voice was as clear as a bell. She enchanted the crowd, and the guards fell back. De la Cruz joined in the song, still trying to snatch the photo back from her.

At the end of the song, Mamá Imelda still had the picture. She ran into Héctor's arms, then gave Miguel the photo and held up a glowing marigold petal.

'Miguel, I give you my blessing,' she said. 'Go home, put up our photos and never forget how much your family loves you.'

But suddenly, strong hands grabbed Miguel. De la Cruz picked him up and flung him off the building! Héctor's photo fell from Miguel's hand as he tumbled over the edge.

The audience cried out in horror. De la Cruz had forgotten that there were big screens showing everything he did!

Pepita caught Miguel and carried the boy to his ancestors. The audience cheered, and everyone knew the truth at last. Ernesto de la Cruz was a fraud and a crook.

The sun's rays were peering over the horizon.
It was almost sunrise.

'We're both out of time,' Héctor whispered.

'No, no . . . Coco can't forget you!' said Miguel.

Héctor reached for a marigold petal. 'You have
our blessing, Miguel.'

'No conditions,' added Mamá Imelda,
helping Héctor lift the marigold petal.

The petal glowed and . . . WHOOSH!
Miguel was home.

Back in Santa Cecilia, Miguel pelted towards his home,
clutching de la Cruz's guitar. He still had a chance to save Héctor.
   When he reached home, he raced to Mamá Coco's side.
   'I saw your papá,' he said.
   Mamá Coco said nothing. She just stared into space. Then Miguel
strummed the guitar and started to sing 'Remember Me'.

Mamá Coco's eyes brightened
and she almost looked younger.
Her memories were flooding back.
Then she joined in with the song
that her father had written for her.

Afterwards, Mamá Coco pulled out
an old book and showed them a torn
picture of Héctor. She began to tell
stories about her papá to her family.
Miguel smiled. He could help Héctor
after all.

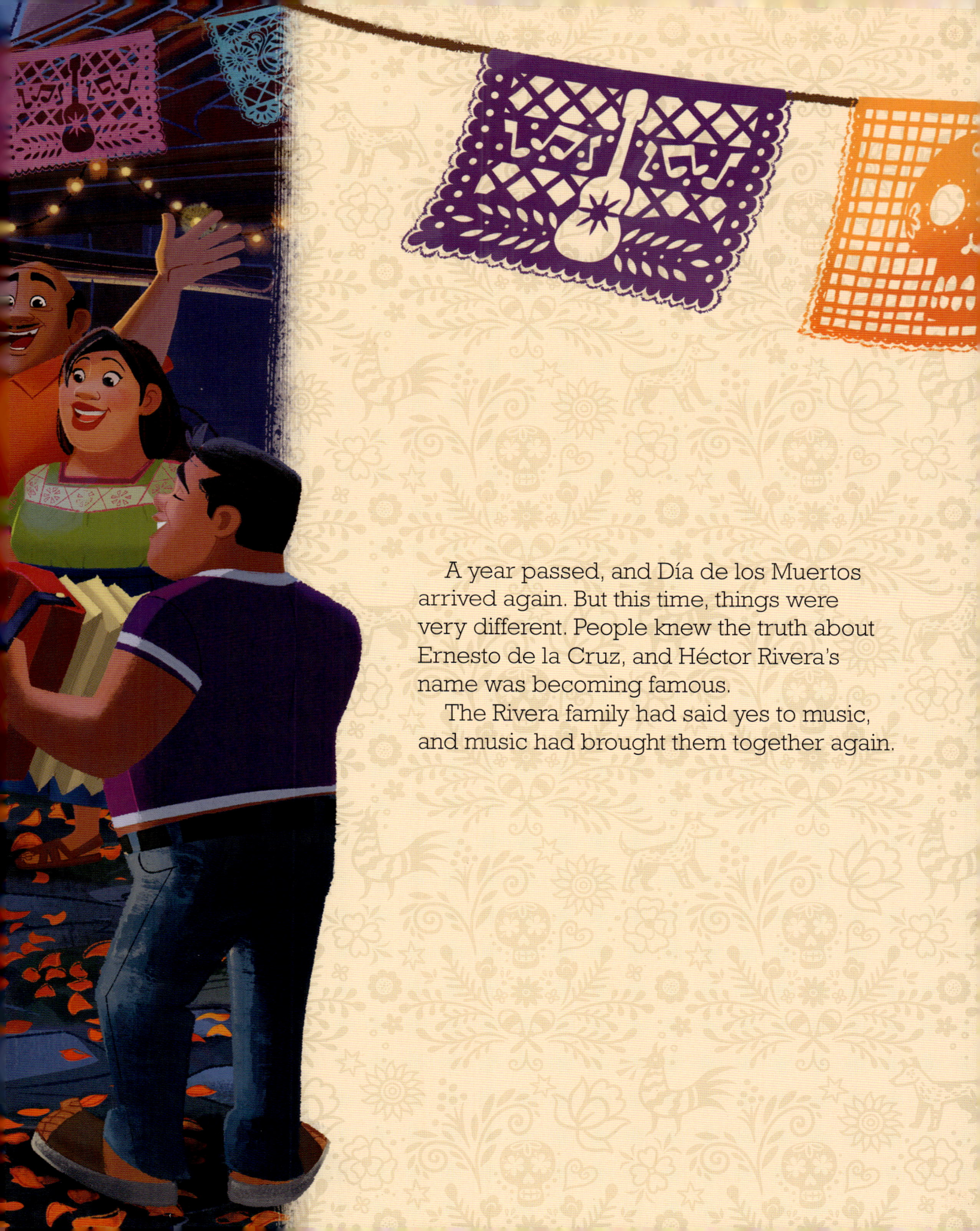

A year passed, and Día de los Muertos arrived again. But this time, things were very different. People knew the truth about Ernesto de la Cruz, and Héctor Rivera's name was becoming famous.

The Rivera family had said yes to music, and music had brought them together again.